# The MYSTERY of SARA BETH

**Follett Publishing Company**

Editorial Offices: Chicago, Illinois

Regional Offices: Chicago, Illinois
Atlanta, Georgia • Dallas, Texas
Sacramento, California • Warrensburg, Missouri

# The MYSTERY OF SARA BETH

Polly Putnam

Illustrated by Judith Friedman

**Library of Congress Cataloging in Publication Data**

Putnam, Polly.
  The mystery of Sara Beth.

  Summary: By carefully observing the behavior of the new girl in her class, Becky discovers why Sara Beth hasn't been very friendly.
  [1. Twins—Fiction. 2. School stories] I. Friedman, Judi, 1935–  . II. Title.
PZ7.P9823My    [E]      81–3282
ISBN 0–695–41628–6      AACR2
ISBN 0–695–31628–1 (pbk.)


Third Printing

# The Mystery Begins

The mystery began in December. Becky and her friends were working. Wind and snow blew against the windows.

The door opened. A girl walked in with
her mother. They stood near the door.
The girl wore a furry blue coat.

Miss Harris, the teacher, spoke to them.
Then she said, "Class, this is our new
girl. Her name is Sara Beth."

Miss Harris pointed to the desk in front
of Becky. "Sit there, Sara Beth,"
Miss Harris said.

Becky smiled when Sara Beth sat down,
but Sara Beth didn't smile back. Sara
Beth didn't turn around all morning.

At noon Becky showed Sara Beth the lunchroom. "Will you eat with us?" Becky asked.

Sara Beth shook her head. She went to a table by herself.

Becky and her friends sat at a table together. They talked about Sara Beth.

"Why doesn't she want to make friends?" asked Becky.

"Maybe she is shy," said David.

"Yes," said Janie. "If we're nice to her, she'll soon be our friend."

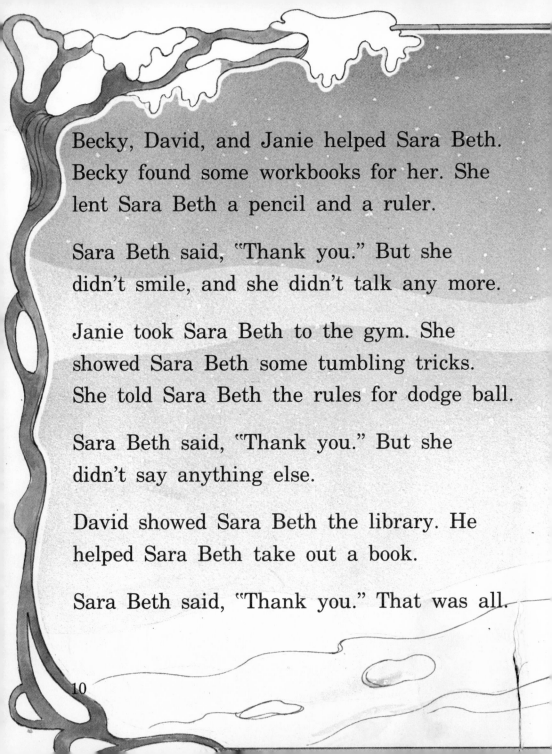

Becky, David, and Janie helped Sara Beth. Becky found some workbooks for her. She lent Sara Beth a pencil and a ruler.

Sara Beth said, "Thank you." But she didn't smile, and she didn't talk any more.

Janie took Sara Beth to the gym. She showed Sara Beth some tumbling tricks. She told Sara Beth the rules for dodge ball.

Sara Beth said, "Thank you." But she didn't say anything else.

David showed Sara Beth the library. He helped Sara Beth take out a book.

Sara Beth said, "Thank you." That was all.

"I give up," said Janie after a few days.
"Sara Beth doesn't want any friends."

"I want to know why," said Becky.
"Everyone wants friends."

11

# Becky Is Puzzled

Becky wanted to solve the mystery of Sara Beth. She wanted to know why Sara Beth didn't want friends. So she looked for clues.

Becky saw that Sara Beth's blue jeans were old and faded. She saw that Sara Beth had only two blouses.

But Sara Beth wasn't the only one who wore faded jeans. And her blouses were always clean and neat. No, Sara Beth's clothes were not a clue to the mystery.

12

Becky had another idea. Maybe Sara Beth was afraid she couldn't do her schoolwork.

Becky peeked at Sara Beth's papers. They said **Good** and had only a few red marks on them.

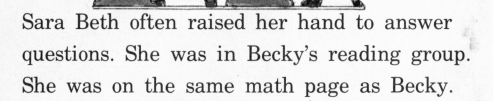

Sara Beth often raised her hand to answer questions. She was in Becky's reading group. She was on the same math page as Becky.

No, Sara Beth wasn't worried about her schoolwork. What other reason could Sara Beth have for being unfriendly? Becky couldn't guess. Sara Beth stayed alone.

Sara Beth stayed alone until the day Miss
Harris carried a big wire cage into the
classroom. The teacher put the cage on
the worktable.

The children crowded around the table.
They looked in the cage and saw two
guinea pigs. One was black, and the other
one was brown and white.

The children were happy to have two new
pets. They named the guinea pigs Harriet
and Smitty.

"Someone will have to help feed and care
for the guinea pigs each day of the week,"
said Miss Harris. "Mondays and Thursdays
will be the hardest days because the cage
will have to be cleaned on those days."

"I'll help," said
Sara Beth. "I'll
do it every
Monday."

16

The next Monday Sara Beth cleaned the cage.
She washed it inside and out. She put
down clean newspapers and hay. She filled
the bottle with fresh water, and she set out
new food. She fed bits of celery and
lettuce to the guinea pigs.

Then Sara Beth let Harriet and Smitty
play on the worktable. She laughed when
Harriet tried to hide under an open book.
She picked up Smitty and held him close
while she petted him.

Becky was more puzzled than ever. Why
would Sara Beth make friends with animals
and not with her classmates?

# Becky Sees Three Clues

During the next few days, three strange things happened. They gave Becky the clues she wanted.

The first strange thing happened in the coatroom after school. Becky was alone with Sara Beth. A reading book dropped to the floor. Sara Beth had hidden it under her coat.

Becky said, "You know Miss Harris doesn't let us take reading books home. She's afraid they will be lost."

19

Sara Beth's face turned red. "Please don't tell," she said.

Becky didn't tell. But she had her first clue.

The second strange thing happened when George Pitt had his birthday party in school. Mrs. Pitt gave everyone a glass of punch. Then she gave everyone a beautiful pink cupcake.

Sara Beth drank her punch. But she didn't eat her cupcake. She wrapped it in her napkin. Then she put it in her desk.

Becky had her second clue.

The third strange thing happened on a Thursday. It was Janie's day to clean the guinea pig cage.

While Janie was cleaning the cage, Harriet jumped off the worktable. She ran under the desks. She ran up one row and down another.

All the children tried to catch her. Everyone was laughing and shouting. The classroom was in an uproar.

Becky was the only one watching Sara Beth. Sara Beth wasn't chasing Harriet.

Sara Beth was standing on a chair. Her face was white, and she was shaking. She was afraid!

Becky had her third clue. It was the strangest of all.

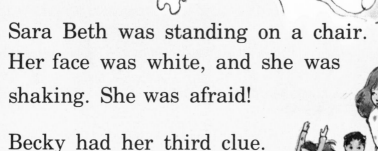

Becky thought about the three clues.

    1. Sara Beth did not obey the rule about taking reading books home.

    2. Sara Beth saved her cupcake instead of eating it.

    3. Sometimes Sara Beth loved guinea pigs, and sometimes she was afraid of them.

All at once Becky solved the mystery! She knew why Sara Beth would not make friends.

23

# One Mystery Is Solved

Becky could hardly wait for the chance to see Sara Beth alone.

At lunchtime Becky sat at Sara Beth's table. Right away Janie and David sat down near them. Becky ate her lunch and said nothing. The mystery would have to wait.

Before gym Becky and Sara Beth were alone in the locker room. Becky started to speak. Then Miss Rogers, the gym teacher, came in. "Hurry up, girls," she said.

Sara Beth followed Miss Rogers out the door.

Becky was afraid she would never see Sara Beth alone. Her luck changed during art.

Miss Harris said, "Becky and Sara Beth, please go to the workroom to get more paper and paint."

Inside the workroom, Sara Beth reached for a jar of paint.

"Tell me," said Becky. "Are you Sara, or are you Beth?"

Sara Beth almost dropped the paint. "What do you mean?" she asked.

26

"I know you're a twin," said Becky. "And I know the two of you take turns coming to school."

Sara Beth's eyes opened wide. "It's true," she said. "How did you know?"

Becky said, "You gave me some clues. I guessed that the reading book and the cupcake were going home to someone. I didn't know who until today when you jumped up in the chair. You are afraid of Harriet. Your twin is not."

27

Sara Beth sat down on a low stool. "I'm Beth," she said. "I was bitten by a guinea pig at our other school. I had to have a tetanus shot. And now I have given away the secret."

Beth put her head in her hands. Becky put her arm around her.

"You were unfriendly so no one would find out the truth," said Becky.

"Yes," said Beth.

"But I don't understand," said Becky. "Why couldn't you both come to school?"

"We have just moved from a place where the weather is not so cold," said Beth. "My father has been out of work. There was money to buy only one warm coat. Sara and I take turns wearing it."

Becky went to the door. "Let's go back to class," she said. "After school we'll tell Miss Harris. She'll know what to do."

"I'm afraid she'll be angry," said Beth.

Miss Harris wasn't angry. "We'll speak
to the school nurse, Beth," she said.
"She keeps extra mittens and hats. Maybe
she has an extra coat."

Beth looked surprised. "You mean there are
other children without warm clothes?" she
asked.

Miss Harris smiled. "Of course," she said.

The next day two smiling girls walked into Becky's classroom. One was wearing a furry blue coat. The other was wearing a brown wool coat.

Now Becky had a new mystery to solve. Which girl was Sara, and which girl was Beth?

**Polly Putnam,** a former school librarian, is a free-lance writer of short stories and books for children.

In addition to giving practice with words that most children will recognize, *The Mystery of Sara Beth* uses the 74 enrichment words listed below.

| | | | |
|---|---|---|---|
| art | extra | napkin | solve(d) |
| | | neat | stool |
| bitten | faded | nice | |
| blew | fresh | noon | tetanus |
| blouses | furry | nurse | third |
| bottle | | | true |
| | group | obey | truth |
| celery | guinea | | tumbling |
| chance | gym | pointed | |
| changed | | punch | unfriendly |
| chasing | hay | puzzled | uproar |
| classmates | | | |
| classroom | idea | raised | weather |
| close | | reason | wind |
| clothes | jeans | rule | wire |
| clue | | | wool |
| coatroom | lent | schoolwork | wore |
| course | lettuce | secret | workbooks |
| crowded | locker | shaking | workroom |
| cupcake | lunchroom | shot | worktable |
| | lunchtime | shouting | worried |
| dodge | | shy | wrapped |
| during | math | | |
| | mystery | | |